RICHARD ADAMS

THE ADVENTURES OF
EGG BOX DRAGON

illustrated by Alex T. Smith

Egg Box Dragon was made out of cut-up egg boxes glued together. His tail was cardboard and the sharp point at the end was painted red to show it was dangerous.

His body was painted green, blue and grey and his eyes were made of shiny bicycle reflectors. His wings were black bin liners and his claws were made out of thick wire.

When Emma brought him home,
everyone admired him enormously.

The local gardener, a normally silent person, said,
"Ah, you mark my words, that critter's got magic."

"How do you know?" asked Emma.

"Find out for yourself tonight – put him to sleep
under the moon and watch what happens."

So Egg Box Dragon was put to bed under the moon.

Next morning, there was a fearful
racket outside in the rose bushes.

It was Egg Box Dragon.

He'd already left paw prints
in the grass and Emma could
hear him roaring…

ROAR!

Egg Box Dragon was perfectly friendly –
but he was a bit mischievous. While Emma
wasn't looking, he ate her breakfast.

Then he climbed into Emma's dad's
coat pocket and burnt a hole.

When everyone calmed down, he went into the garden and practised breathing fire, terrifying the next-door cat.

When Emma got home from school,
she found her dad searching all over the
place. "What have you lost?" she asked.

"My reading glasses," he said.

"They're outside," Egg Box Dragon roared.
"On the grass."

"On the grass?" said Emma's dad.
"Where?"

"By the rrrrrose bushes! Go and look!"

And they were.

It turned out that Egg Box Dragon was able to find just about anything.

When Emma's mum couldn't find her lipstick, Egg Box Dragon said, "It's on top of the rrrradio!"

When Mrs Hapgood, who lived next door, couldn't find her tortoise, Egg Box Dragon thought and thought, bashing his cardboard tail on the tortoise's house.

Then he lifted up a branch of the hedge and revealed the sleeping tortoise.

Soon, everyone knew about
Egg Box Dragon.

When Tom from two doors down
lost his football, Egg Box Dragon
rescued it from the top of a tree.

When Jane Clacy lost her purse
with the money for her school
trip, Egg Box Dragon found it
behind the piano, where the cat
had been playing with it.

Then Mrs Forsyth, who ran the
village shop, lost her keys.

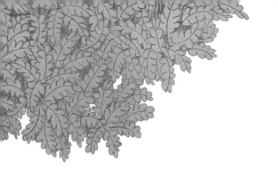

"You left them beside the washbasin in your bathroom," Egg Box Dragon said.

Mrs Forsyth was delighted and told all her customers.

Soon the newspapers got to hear about
Egg Box Dragon and he was on the TV news.

EGG BOX
DRAGON SAVES
THE DAY
(AGAIN!)

The ROYAL TIMES

Even the Queen got to hear about Egg Box Dragon.
She was planning a big tea party and princes and
princesses were coming from all over the world to visit.

But when she put her crown on, she discovered that
the biggest and brightest diamond was missing!

The Queen was very worried and sent a royal car to
Emma's home to ask for Egg Box Dragon's help.

Emma and her dad and Egg Box Dragon felt rather nervous, but the Queen welcomed them most royally and explained what had happened.

Egg Box Dragon thought and thought. He looked at the window, which was open, just a tiny bit. Then he said, "The diamond has flown out of the room."

The Queen's guards said Egg Box Dragon must be crazy, especially when he began to breathe fire and roar, "I'm not wrrrong! Look outside!"

Emma and her dad ran to the window. They hoped Egg Box Dragon hadn't made a mistake.

The Queen looked through her royal binoculars
at the tall trees outside the palace window. She
ordered her guards to bring some tall ladders.

Then they climbed up and up and up and found...

...the diamond in a magpie's nest!

The Queen was delighted to have her diamond back. And she was very pleased with Egg Box Dragon. She gave him a special medal of his own.

Soon it was time for tea and all kinds of
important people started arriving. They
looked magnificent in their robes and tiaras.

But the biggest and best crown belonged to
the Queen and the diamond shone out royally.

Emma and her dad tucked into
toasted teacakes, tea and tiny scones.
Egg Box Dragon ate a whole chocolate
cake, which he melted himself.

Later, Emma and her dad were driven home in the royal car and Egg Box Dragon was so proud of himself that he roared all the way.

So Egg Box Dragon became a hero although there was a bit of trouble…

...when the Queen found a huge burn in the royal hedge!

For Lesley Young who insisted this story be told – R. A.
and
For William Singh, and his Mummy and Daddy
and big sister Margaret – A.T.S.

First published in Great Britain in 2017 by Hodder Children's Books
This paperback edition published in 2018

A catalogue record for this book is available from the British Library

978 1 444 93841 8

Printed and bound in China

An imprint of Hachette Children's Group
Part of Hodder and Stoughton
Carmelite House, 50 Victoria Embankment, London EC4Y 0DZ

An Hachette UK Company
www.hachette.co.uk

www.hachettechildrens.co.uk

Dear Reader,

One nice sunny afternoon, when Dad was 93 and having a good day, I brought him a pad of paper and his favourite fountain pen and asked him to write down Egg Box Dragon. At the end of the day, he handed me his story.

He first thought of Egg Box Dragon more than four decades ago after I told him about a school art project. We never actually got round to making our dragon in class but the idea triggered something in Dad's mind.

Egg Box Dragon then joined Hazel, Fiver and Bigwig, the stars of Watership Down, in entertaining me and my sister Ros on long car journeys. My Dad was never short of a story and told them as we drove.

Dad was absolutely enchanted by Alex T. Smith's beautiful illustrations as, indeed, are we. We hope you enjoy the story as much as we did when we were children.

JULIET JOHNSON